# The Bone Killer:

# An Electrifying Thriller of Suspense and Mystery

# Gian Marcos

*For Ale who changed my world.*

*"They say I have shed innocent blood...but what is the use of blood if not to be shed?"*

**Candyman**

# Foreword

It was an unmarked car, a black Nissan Sentra with a few decades on it, right in the middle of the parking lot of the largest shopping mall in Columbia Washington. Dozens of police officers could be seen cordoning off the area with yellow tape. From a distance, it might seem like just another homicide, but the astonishment on the faces of some detectives nearby indicated that it had to do with something more sinister than a simple murder.

# Index

# Panic

Washington, D.C. November 12 6:12 A.M.

It was an unmarked car, a black Nissan Sentra with a few decades on it, right in the middle of the parking lot of the largest shopping mall in Columbia Washington. All around, dozens of police officers could be seen cordoning off the area with yellow tape. From a distance you might think it was just another homicide, but the astonishment on the faces of some of the detectives nearby indicated that it had to do with something more sinister than a simple murder.

-Oh, my goodness! I think I'm going to throw up," said Officer Tom Logan just half a meter away from the female corpse inside the Nissan. Off to the side was Chief Inspector Richard Martel drawing deductions and poring over parts of the car, as if trying to visualize the whole scene.

-Whoever committed this brutality is beyond hate," he commented, immediately walking away to the back of the car as Lisa Owen, the head of the forensic criminology department, arrived.

- Well, here you are at last," the inspector muttered to himself, "we were waiting for you, we couldn't leave without you doing your job.

She waved at him and made a little friendly face as she advanced towards the Nissan about ten feet away, and then exclaimed- it was a tiring night for the second shift, just finished leaving another crime scene, and....

Richard found the impression he saw on Owen's face too much when he passed through the agents accompanying Tom. Naturally, it was not a normal reaction, because, although the woman's body looked terrible, Lisa had more than six years of experience and that should not have put her like that, but what she immediately expressed stunned the two inspectors.

-It can't be," he said in a loud tone. -What's going on? -A chorus was immediately heard behind him while on the other side of the vehicle some forensic assistants were already doing their work trying to gather evidence around them.

-Undoubtedly, the girl who was murdered under the bridge where I come from has the same marks and signs of torture on her body... and I see that she was killed in the same atrocious and cruel manner.

-I was told about a murder on the west side when I arrived at the office, Inspector Mark is the one who did it, but I never imagined that..." Richard commented without finishing the sentence.

-Everything indicates that this is... a serial killer," Tom said hesitantly.

-It's too early to tell, we'll see," replied Lisa, as she ordered all the police officers and inspectors to stand back and let them work.

Richard and company kept their distance outside the circle of yellow ribbons, looking expectantly, while the forensic scientist and her team collected the most obvious evidence that would give some clue to the perpetrators of such an unusual crime, then in the laboratory they would check the vehicle in depth.

Inside the old car one could glimpse a naked female body bound head and foot with strange marks all over her body, as if they had been inflicted by some kind of hot coals and knife cuts. His neck was completely broken backwards. The face, although swollen, still showed an indescribable horror as a result of the humiliations and tortures inflicted by the murderer. Although it showed traces of torture and dismemberment, there was something unusual at first sight: it was a metal rod that pierced her anally and protruded a few centimeters from the side of her mouth. It was a chilling scene, a rare sight in the history of the city, let alone for Inspector Richard and his colleague.

-Tom Logan, a 33 year old police officer who looked calmer after such an unexpected first impression, said, "Do you have any idea, Chief. Richard did not respond with words, he just shook his head slightly, his thoughts were set in motion, asking and answering himself in his mind how to solve this mysterious and difficult looking case. Two deaths in the same way indicated that it was not a simple murder product of a robbery, or a settling of scores for money, because from experience, that is not usually done to people for reasons of that nature. Although, it could also be the product of a sick mind, but that was the crux of the case.

-We have to solve this case, otherwise the pressure will be on our heads," commented Inspector Tom suddenly and another agent on the left side taking protocol notes nodded. Then Richard added.

-It's not for nothing that we are in the most important city in the world and in the sector that involves the white house and the president, and you know, if cases like this keep happening, in a few days our heads will be on television explaining why we can't find the person responsible. I just hope Dr. Owen gives us some clues, though....

Just as he was about to finish his dissertation, a call from his cell phone suddenly interrupted him, he immediately answered and an unknown voice in a whisper was heard repeating a phrase: "I know who it is, it's him... I know who it is, it's him...". Before he could reply, the stranger hung up, leaving the detective dumbfounded.

-What's going on? Don't tell me it's Dilan the boss," his partner asked, and he shook his head.

- Then why are you making that face? Don't tell me your girlfriend already scolded you so early.

-No no, it's nothing like that... You're not going to believe it," he replied as he passed saliva and paused to glance over to where forensics was, then answered dryly, looking at Tom. - a call from a male voice who knows who it was.

-What! But how does he know the number..." commented Logan giving a fleeting glance towards the avenue of hundreds of cars that were probably heading to work. As if somehow thinking that the killer or whoever had called his partner was there in the middle of the traffic jam stalking them. Although, to tell the truth, it was just an unsubstantiated idea.

-I don't know..., but we have to take this phone to the IT department, although it is a private number, Bobby the specialist in this will know where the call came from at least. I think we have to go, and then the doctor will send us the report if there is any news or we go through it.

Tom nodded and they immediately alerted the coroner and gave some orders to some of their subordinate agents to follow up on the crime scene.

There was not much to think about, he had to act immediately, because beyond deducing that those female deaths could be a settling of scores for money or drugs, the way they were executed could also point to the fact that it could be the product of a psychopath in the southern sector of the city where they were located; the most important area because of what was involved in the Capitol, Casablanca and Congress. And if that spread, there would be a lot of pressure for the police investigation area that Richard represented in that area. Besides, it did not suit him, because he was planning to fight for a seat in the Columbia State Senate in the House of Congress, and if the case was not solved soon, it could affect him in the public scrutiny.

Richard, 38 years old, was a decorated former military officer who had gone from strategic missions in the military to the police force when he was only 27, and from there in the following decade he made a name for himself in the field for his great ability to solve cases and keep the city in relative safety. This unusual crime of the two women was something that alerted the corps he represented, because there was only one murder every three days in the entire city. With an average of 180 per year. But the way in which they were executed and the distance of three kilometers between the two gave much to think about.

**Columbia Corps Central Office of Computer Intelligence Washington November 13 11:24 AM**

-I hope you have good news for me," shouted Martel, who was leaning on the reception desk of the computer intelligence area where Bobby, 45 years old, was in charge, and who was already on the other side waiting for them and told them to go through a tempered glass door, and then both colleagues followed him to his office a few meters further down the hall. Before sitting down at his large oval table, he said, "I am glad you are here, it has been a while since you were here, let's go! Sit down, I have some interesting information about the phone you left yesterday.

Martel and Owen then took their seats a little anxious to know the origin of that mysterious call that could possibly be related to the fateful crime perpetrated the night before.

-Something a bit unusual Richard," Bobby commented as he analyzed some data on a series of computers in front of him, and then proffered, "the person who called your number according to the data that was recorded on your cell phone, came exactly from pay phone #424 which is located 65 meters from the Washington National Cathedral... mmm we're talking about fifteen minutes from here.

-Curious, do you think he could be the killer? -Logan asked without specifying who.

-I don't know, it's your job," Bobby replied in a joking tone, as he used to get along with him.

-He was careful because it was not even more than twelve seconds, he was afraid of being tracked down. -The cybersecurity expert added.

-Then we don't have anything concrete," said Richard in a tone that was to be expected.

-No no, I have something better," he replied as he pointed to a huge screen behind the two inspectors as they turned their necks to see what was being displayed on the screen.

-Who is it? -asked Logan.

-The one who made the call," replied the engineer.

-What! -Richard exclaimed.

-It is very typical in cases of this type that those involved use public phones, so for obvious reasons I accessed the cameras in the area where the call came from, and there was only that one, public phone #424... and for obvious reasons there right in front of the Washington National Church there was a surveillance camera and..., unfortunately as you can see in the video it only shows his diffuse back, because that big tree in front of the camera saved him from being completely identified," he said.

-At least we know he's a middle-aged guy from his build," added Logan.

Richard looked at him and continued -del...gado, white skin, we don't have much, but, worse is nothing, -thanks! we'll still take the report, and the video you send it to the mail -he said as he stood up and took the document to head for the exit, Logan fist bumped Bobby as he threw a joking comment and left.

Even though it wasn't a lot of information that would help to quickly identify the killer, they knew that it was worse than nothing, so they immediately went to the forensic department where Dr. Lisa had called them to give them the news and to start putting the case together.

**Police Forensic Science Department Columbia Washington 12:00 pm**

With no one else but her in the middle of that huge facility where all kinds of scientific apparatus and objects for analysis and experimentation could be observed, Lisa Owen was waiting for them, showing her slightly frustrated face. Perhaps, due to the little evidence that the corpse yielded.

Lisa Owen had been head of the forensic science department of the Columbia Police Department for six years, but she had barely been at the helm for a year when she turned thirty-three. Richard walked over and greeted her by voice, Owen did the same. She wore her trademark bonnet, glasses on her head and an all-white suit, typical of forensic scientists.

-What do you have for us doctor? -Richard broke the ice in a somewhat indifferent tone of voice, but Lisa was used to guys like him who were not to her liking because of the black history of having a reputation of executing them before arresting them. Even if it was purely a myth about him without any proof. Lisa never wanted to be friends with Martel when it was presented to them that they were going to work together years ago and would always see each other at crime scenes. Despite his black record, what she disliked most was his tone of voice and his rough, unkempt, uncouth demeanor, although she had no choice but to do her duty. However, perhaps her main apathy on his part was due in the first instance to the fact that when they met, he wanted to somehow establish a friendship beyond the professional, and she stopped him in his tracks, and from those days she may have expected some animosity, and that's why she was so cold towards him. However, that was worth cheese to her.

-The person who carried it out was too clever in leaving no trace but one. -The coroner said as the two detectives looked at each other suspiciously for a moment to hear the rest. Then she paused and went to some lockers of filing cabinets at the back, took one out and came back again, immediately reading the report a little ahead of time, which surprised Richard.

-The girl's name was Karla Davison, 28 years old, single mother, worked for the McDonald's on the corner of Omega Street on the late night shift. So, at my deduction, somewhere between Omega Street and Maret School where there is a lonely stretch of at least 300 yards under a bridge, she was attacked. Someone gagged her, hit her in the parietal area... She was walking that stretch because her house was 600 meters from the establishment and that was the area she was walking according to her ID. She presented a strong contusion in the parietal area, but it was not life-threatening. By inference the perpetrator wanted her alive, so he made sure to knock her unconscious. What he did next was terrible...- he added with a slight pause, passed some saliva and then continued -she was raped anally and vaginally, but it did not end there, the two girls presented the same, on the same night both of them had most of their front teeth forcibly removed with tweezers, not having enough, the sick man or whoever did this, cut her nipples, presented blows and bruises on thighs, arms and neck...it is superfluous to present the corpse to you again. Once she was raped, she was tortured with a metallic object at hundreds of degrees centigrade, which was then introduced inches from her vagina.

-I don't want to hear everything," said Richard a little desperate, he only cared about the evidence, although those data were protocol, according to him they didn't help much to find the suspect. - Hurry up Lisa, we have to go - he added a little bit angry.

-It's the rules, detective," she replied in a scathing tone.

-Come on, finish! -he replied, somewhat annoyed inwardly. He didn't like to be contradicted, but he had no jurisdiction in the area of forensic science. Despite being respected, he had to abide by the rules.

-After torturing them, he apparently strangled them and broke their necks, probably by twisting them, to the extent that the c7 vertebrae in the neck area were shattered. Then to deductions, due to the excess of liquid found in the vaginal cavity, the subject introduced a pressurized water hose, probably with the objective of eliminating any trace of seminal fluid that had been left. The degenerate did not even bother to use a condom. Then he cleaned the body because ethylic traces were found in different areas of the body. Finally, not taking with the atrocities; he introduced surely when they lay lifeless a red-hot metal rod through the anus until he found the opening through the mouth, both women suffered as never before. We did not find skin or traces of semen of the author, but never a crime is perfect, because fortunately we found a strand of brown hair coming surely from the murderer, - he concluded, leaving astonished both investigators. They were sure of one thing, that the guy responsible was a son of a bitch and they had to hunt him down no matter what.

-Well," exclaimed Richard, clenching his fist slightly, already eager to get the bastard and earn points for his campaign that would surely take place at some point in the summer of next year. Surely because of his fame in the city in the security field; he would win easily.

-And what can we do with a hair! I don't think there's much to it," he exclaimed annoyed just to contradict her, he knew it was his job to find more real clues, so they left the science department with the ID of Karla, the McDonald's employee because there were no traces or information from relatives of the other executed woman. What the doctor did not tell her at that moment was that in the next few hours they would analyze with some chemist colleagues the origin and age range of the hair strand, as well as compare them with the DNA bank of convicts and ex-convicts from all over the country in case any of them matched. So if they were lucky they would be able to deduce the age range, sex and some extra data that would help confirm if there were any suspects and be able to compare the DNA. I was just waiting for the corps of inspectors and detectives to gather something else.

As expected, the news spread like wildfire throughout the District of Columbia, causing commotion and panic. The report of the local public safety chief John Spencer at first mentioned to the press: "that it was a settling of scores between gangsters", but obviously, this was quickly changed by the pressure of Karla Davison's relatives appealing that this was totally false and that it was all about a psychopathic maniac who deprived her life because he looked at her helpless when she was walking home from work about 600 meters away. The Davison family was quick to file a lawsuit with the board and controllers alleging that they had sullied the reputation and honor of their family by accusing him of things that had nothing to do with their daughter.

Hours later on the 9 p.m. evening news, Columbia's head of security John Spencer was removed from his post. And the official version that was handled was that the two girls Karla Davison, 28 years old, single mother and cashier of McDonald's on Omega Street Avenue and a female named Ana, around 24 years old, in a street situation, were brutally murdered the night of Thursday, November 11 by an unknown person, that so far there were no concrete reports of the perpetrator, but that they were working at full speed in the investigations to find the alleged murderer. Such was the collective euphoria and panic in the following hours that the President of the United States himself, Bill Lambert, said a few words to calm the collective psychosis, condemning such a heartless act, and promising that those responsible would be punished to the full extent of the law.

# The search



A mood of melancholy and sadness prevailed in the Davison's small residence. They had already gone from grief and despair to painful resignation. Karla's mother lay in the middle of the living room hugging her husband. Detectives Richard Martel and Tom Logan were just beginning the interrogation to find out everything about their daughter, and at least give them a clue as to where to direct the investigation. On the other hand, a couple of kilometers away from where the other girl who appeared to be living on the street was found, homicide inspector Mark was investigating under the bridges to gather a little more information about the deceased and why she was brutally murdered, and what relationship she might have shared with Karla Davison. But he's not likely to find anything.

-Mrs. Belly, we are very sorry for the loss of your daughter. We don't want to be impertinent, we only want to do justice for your daughter. So whatever you think or believe might help solve the crime, don't hold anything back," said Richard as he exchanged glances with Karla's father. They both nodded in approval and then continued with the interrogation, taking note of anything important...

-Tell us a little about your daughter, Mrs. Belly.

-I don't know how to begin, detective," he replied in a melancholy voice.

-We know she was a single mother, do you know if she was currently in a romantic relationship?

-No no," replied his father forcefully, both detectives looked at him in astonishment at the unusual reaction giving a tinge at times of anger.

-No, since my daughter left her ex a lazy bastard, she never had a love relationship again and he was the only one she had. She wasn't a woman who went around with one or the other like most people do," he declared, paused slightly agitated and then continued, "she was a nice lady, I don't know why a damned bastard did that to my little girl.

Richard looked at Tom somewhat astonished at the energetic scene that was to be expected from Mr. Peterson, who looked in righteous tones like pastors condemning sinners. -lu...ego left that idler and came to live with us....

-Can you give us the name of your daughter's ex-husband and address," Logan asked as he wrote it down in a notebook.

— So Brandon Brown lives on the High Street across town, right?

— They both shook their heads, although to tell the truth, Mr. Peterson was the one Mr. Peterson suspected the least, since Brandon, although he was a slacker, did not believe him capable of such savagery. He was never known to be violent or jealous, in fact, the reason for the separation was an infidelity on his part, so for obvious reasons his in-laws did not suspect him. However, the line of investigation was open to different suspects.

— Friends you visited...?

— No detective, my daughter didn't go out anywhere, it was from work to home and from home to work. She only spent time with the child and nothing else, - whispered her mother with a crestfallen face, her husband interrupted her and added - she was shy, we don't have anyone in mind that would want to hurt my child, she got along with everyone and never got into trouble. - She said, then her eyes sparkled with feelings, then Logan asked the next question and then another and another:

— Any debts or enemies the family has?

— No no, we are a religious family we have never had any problems with anyone or debts, so nothing like that.

— I understand Mr. Peterson. Any close family members who have had contact with Karla in the last few hours or ...

— Our whole family lives in Austin Texas, we don't have anyone here," replied Mrs. Belly.

At that moment Richard knew that this information would be enough, then as the investigation progressed, if they needed it, they would come back for more information. So they immediately went to the McDonald's establishment where Karla Davison had worked for the last two years to gather information and make the case more conclusive.

**Somewhere in Columbia Washington inside the moving car.**

-Hey Bobby.

-What is it Richard? -They found something.

-Not yet, but I want to ask you something, can you check if there are any cameras on Omega Street and Maret School, probably where Karla was attacked... Precisely in that area is where there is a huge bridge and a stretch that she used to walk every day to go to work.

-Of course, I'll let you know in a few hours if I find anything.

-Thanks buddy, I owe you one," Martel commented as he turned the corner and arrived at the famous fast food establishment. An hour after interviewing most of the people on the late night shift where Karla worked: they left somewhat disappointed. But not before walking the same route Karla had walked two days earlier. So, although tired, they would have the opportunity to walk the same route that the 28-year-old had walked before she was murdered.

-We're stuck," Logan said as he pulled out a cigarette and lit it, visibly somewhat stressed. -There's not much to go on except that hair to lead us to the culprit. Hopefully Bobby has something for us.

-The girl left at 6:30... for where we are now she must have arrived at 6:40, it's about 500 meters from here to that street in the background where her neighborhood is. So in this lonely area under this bridge was surely where she was attacked by someone," commented the detective looking around him where two roads converged, not very busy for those hours yet, and much more for the late night hours. He turned to all sides trying to look for any clue that would give him at least something to continue the investigation.

- The guy according to him is middle-aged, most likely a crazy rapist," hinted Logan to the side of him.

-We're stuck, but I can't find any other explanation than that the guy attacked her here between this section as the coroner said," Richard mumbled as he walked a long way under the bridge and reached another avenue where there was a lot of traffic, and where it would be unlikely that at 6:46 pm, which was probably the time it took her to get from McDonald's to the intersection of the avenue, she would have been mugged by a moving car. A hypothesis that they discarded due to the fact that that same afternoon they went to the same place to check the traffic and indeed, it was too much for any person to have noticed a kidnapping.

**2:13 p.m. on the third day at the home of Brandon Brown, ex-husband of Karla Davison.**

-Damn it! Bobby didn't find any security cameras in the area, or any suspects coming out of that cross street intersection where the last camera she passed by was and recorded everything that day just off the avenue..." said Richard as he sped down High Street east of the city.

-It's more complicated than I thought -refuted his partner with his eyes to the side as he turned on the radio, and as expected the same news of Karla Davison resounded on 98.3 am: "In other news, according to the police department, the girl was murdered in the early hours of November 12, according to the prosecutor several lines of investigation are being handled..."

-Put that shit down, will you! - replied Richard with his eyes straight ahead, "lines of investigation, can't you see we can't move forward and that new prosecutor son of a bitch is always sticking his nose in.

Logan nodded and sketched a smile as he lit a cigarette and switched her to the station to drop her off at 98 .4 where Scorpion's song "Wind Of Change" was playing.

-That's much better," added the chief as he turned onto 8th onto San Bernardino Street where Brandon Brown ex of Karla Davison should be, but just as he was doing that a radio call from subordinate agent Mark across town stunned him.

-Hey Richard you're not going to believe this, but....
-Tell me, what's going on now, man? -he answered as Logan lowered the volume of the music.

-Two corpses in the same shape as two days ago were found just a few hours ago... apparently they were left in the early morning, a homeless man found them under the bridge, then people alerted the police, here I am at the scene with Dr. Owen and company.

-Holy cow," replied the chief inspector as he stopped the car and pulled into the street. He thought of something, and instead of arriving at young Brandon Brown's residence as planned, he turned around. He knew that the killer whoever it was was not that wretched fellow, it would have to be someone else, and the investigations would naturally have to be directed elsewhere.

The fact is that without any clue that would lead them to the culprit, the case was becoming quite difficult, almost reaching a dead end, and mostly because of the pressure from the higher-ups. Although, in part it was a good thing that he continued to kill, because sooner or later he would leave a clear trail, if not already. The most disturbing thing for Richard was that the murderer was only killing young women, so he should undoubtedly be a sexually ill maniac, but whoever the culprit was, they would have to arrest him in the next few hours, otherwise, because of the way the internal security prosecutor was, their heads could blow off. At that point, different police and forensic analysis stations were carrying out analysis and investigations trying to find the criminal who was provoking this wave of disturbing and sadistic murders.

The news were not long in coming and resounded with greater intensity that same night in the state, even the case of Karla Davison cooled to give way to the next macabre case of two young women, one, Sophie, 17 years old and Monica, 23 years old, both murdered with a difference of two kilometers and equally manacled with a black wire lamp light and brutally tortured with the same tonic of torment as both first victims, where a metal rod was perceived as well through them anally until reaching the mouth. In neither case did they leave cars this time. The murderer probably drove to both sites and left the corpses as if daring justice to find him, if they could.

There was nothing, they hadn't even been able to track down the strange guy who had called them on the first day of the whole case. But, just that night at Richard's residence in his Annandale neighborhood on the west side of the city, a yellow envelope with a brief message inside his yard alarmed him. The document contained the following disturbing note, probably typed with the intention of leaving no loose ends: "Mr. Richard, sorry for the call the other day, you probably think I am the murderer but, no, I just want you to know that I have not been able to sleep thinking that if I say what I saw the other morning my life could be in danger, in due time I will say it if they do not get to him first, but I think I know who is the culprit of all the deaths, hopefully! I hope they catch him before I confess who he is, but believe me, it is something I really don't want to do, because not only will I be in danger but my whole family will be exposed". With that strange message Richard finished reading at about half past six in the afternoon while he took a panoramic look outside from his kitchen as if thinking: "that son of a bitch wants to trick me, I don't believe him, but how the fuck did he know I live here? Immediately after that he went upstairs where his 24/7 ftp recording system was on his security camera that he had just inside his front door that faced exactly the street door to the courtyard where whoever had left the letter would show up in the footage.

After a few minutes of frame-by-frame analysis he realized that the person who carried the package out of the entrance to his property was a child of the Marshall neighbors, and that clearly told him one thing; that the suspect used the child to avoid being caught, because clearly there were no cameras on the main avenue of the neighborhood. But just in case, he requested a warrant to check house by house in the neighborhood for security cameras, but unfortunately with negative results.

**7:45 am fourth day of research**

-You'll tell the boss about the message," Logan exclaimed.

-No, I'll wait. It may be an alibi of the killer, though... he swore it wasn't him, but.

-Those psychopaths are smart, he could be playing with us, I wouldn't trust him, but what I wonder is, why you? There are several inspectors from other corporations investigating the case.

-I don't know," Richard had whispered while passing hot coffee and tasting a chocolate donut. According to the doctor, the subject of the hair found on the body has gray hair at the base, and the brown hair is dyed, so according to her deductions he must be between forty-five and fifty years old.

-That's what the report said," muttered Logan as he got up from his chair and went to get another coffee. Seconds later two women entered the small bar that looked completely empty at about 7 am, and sat down behind Logan and Richard, ordered a coffee and began to chat. At first of banalities, but then the talk drifted and they mentioned something that made both detectives look at each other suspiciously....

I was telling you Kira, the poor girl from the news... I can't remember her name, the one who had a bar shoved up her ass, she worked in front of the bar where I work, and do you know what ? - asked the obese woman while the other one with the sculpted body smiled at the waitress who was about to give her her order. Then she continued, - no tell me.

-That day I met her exactly at the end of the Omega Street bridge, because I entered at seven o'clock and it was about 6:40 pm and she was in her uniform, and just before crossing the corner of the street to pass the section of the bridge where that black car from the news, you won't believe it! passed near me, it was starting to get dark, but I don't remember the guy who was inside, I think he was wearing a black cap and glasses....

-Good heavens, don't tell me," said her friend, somewhat horrified. That scene was particularly special because the perpetrators responsible for the investigation were there by chance, although Detective Richard did not want to bother the two diners at the moment. At the end of breakfast he had to present himself to both women, who had no choice but to accompany them to make their formal statement to the homicide department.

# Suspect



Although the department of investigators, including Richard from the different police stations in Columbia, had put together the case and had some elements to consider, the investigation did not point to a clear suspect, or rather none at that moment. Richard had said nothing to his colleagues except to Logan about the strange message that was left outside his home, and although the sender swore he was not involved in the murders, he was not trustworthy for Martel either.

Fortunately, in the following two weeks there were no homicides with the same characteristics throughout the city, but the investigations, even though they were at a standstill, would have to continue.

That's why on the afternoon of November 28, weeks after finding the first victim, they went to the Washington State Penitentiary on the west side of the city to interview some of the homicide suspects who had been arrested in the last two weeks. They found two suspects; one Ramon Rodriguez who killed a woman and raped her, and the other Daniel Robert who assaulted a young college girl south of the city. However, after a long interview with them of more than an hour, there were no indications of suspicion that they had anything to do with them, but still to rule them out, DNA tests of hair fibers were done and they were negative, so they were acquitted in the case of the femicides of Karla Davison and other victims.

**One week later - Friday evening, 8 p.m. -
Richard Martel Residence**

A lot had happened and the case had gone cold in the city, so it was left in the files. The detectives had other important cases to solve.

But that evening when the detective arrived home someone was waiting for him. He entered a little tired of the routine. He pulled the doorknob and as he closed the door behind him; a gun rested on the back of his neck and the stranger said bitingly.

-You probably think I'm a thief, but don't worry! I'm not going to hurt you, I just want you to sit in the armchair in front of me, don't turn to look at me. - Richard took a few steps to his living room that was in front of him, immediately sat down and exclaimed:

-Come on man! take whatever you want or tell me how much you want? maybe you need money, but you don't have to do this, I'll gladly give it to you.

-I don't want money... I'm not a thief. I'm here to...

At that moment Richard nodded his head as he listened without paying attention to the last sentences the man said, it was him. Thinking back, he remembered the same timbre of the voice of the man who had spoken to him on the phone that November 12 when the first murdered woman was found.

-I think by your reaction, Mr. Richard, you've figured it out," whispered the stranger.

-It's you, tell me what do you want? Why are you here? - asked the detective, trying to make him reason and allow him to turn around. The guy said - no, don't turn around, not yet. Richard stopped trying, and put his head forward again.

-I'm here to tell you what I know, as far as I can see it's been more than fifteen days, and I didn't see on the news that they've caught this guy, which I doubt they will if not....

-Why do you say that? -asked Martel.

-Because it is unlikely that an accusation from a simple citizen like me would get him arrested.

-Tell me, what do you know about the killer?

-Mr. Richard, I know you are a police detective, and believe me, with some research I found your number in the yellow section, it was a bit complicated, but I was there all that night after seeing that scene... you won't believe it, but...

-Speak.

-Promise me that you will not press charges against me and that you will keep my identity hidden," said the subject while shakily wielding the pistol lightly pointed at Richard.

-I promise," said the inspector without thinking.

-I know in advance that many times the same witness of a crime is accused and sentenced and I don't want him to go through that with me.

- If he is innocent I swear to you. But by the way, what is your name?

-Never mind my name, Mr. Richard. Give me your word.

-All right I give you my word, no one will know about you, if all this is true, you will handle yourself as a protected witness no one will know about it I will just say that someone informed me and that's all.

-Well, that's much better," mumbled the stranger as he took a chair that was still next to him and sat down, always holding his gun. -That early morning, November 12th, I was on duty guarding just an area of houses where the works have been stopped, but for obvious reasons they take care of vandals and invaders... the area is on the outskirts of the city, the thing is...

He paused for a moment, perhaps the subject was afraid to say what he was about to confess, an accusation of the caliber he was about to confess, for that man could mean many things. Such an accusation could send him to prison and, in the worst case, end his life. Then by the way he ran his hand over his head, he surely summoned up the extra courage to continue.

- Around that area there is nothing but some abandoned warehouses and at... half a kilometer is when the lighted streets begin, so it seemed quite abnormal to me that a black car, just an old sedan, would arrive at about 1 a.m. that night. It was going at a normal speed on the only dirt road that passes in front of the construction zone. From my experience of having been working the night shift for over eight months in that part, there is no one in those vandalized warehouses, not even the vandals live there, only occasionally in the daytime they use it to get high, but at night no one. So it looked pretty weird to me that a sedan was parked around the back of the warehouses... I looked at a few flashes of light, but then they went out. I don't really know, I thought at first instance they were young people; you know, sex, drugs, because there was a young woman and a guy in a cap. From my distance of about 300 meters I could glimpse something, not much, but because of the headlight of the area I was looking after I could see something up to there, then that guy realized my presence and got into the car and drove to the back of the other warehouse, which was the last and most hidden one, stuck to a grove of bushes. At that moment I said, "they are going to have sex, that's why they don't want strangers". I was probably armed so as not to be afraid of Moors on the coast because if it had been me I would never have been in such a dangerous place, there are gangs you know, always walking in lonely places is a danger and with a girl much more... by that time I said; well, lucky me, you will have sex tonight.... but soon something made my hair stand on end, just when I was about to make my rounds again in the whole area of those unfinished private houses that are about forty, I heard something that made me change my mind; a scream, and it was not of pleasure as you would expect. A scream that was eerily audible due to the null noise of the city, only the night and the trees around. So I said to myself: "God! listen well, that was a noise of; bah! it must be my subconscious that I relate sex with screams", but no Mr. Richard.

The second one was clear "help!", at that moment I wasn't one hundred percent sure whether to call the police or go investigate on my own. Since there are never vandals at night because they know there is security, they no longer send two and I was the only one on duty. I set out to leave the area alone and went out the back way that leads directly to those abandoned warehouses, which are exactly four in number, each about forty meters apart at most, and overgrown with wild grass. So, I grabbed my flashlight and baton and carefully walked towards the area where the car had gone, which I didn't think was very far because there was no road beyond it, since it was the beginning of the reserve. Therefore, I thought that whatever was happening was not something good, although half way there I thought that maybe it was a simple marital quarrel or something like that, but then....When I turned at the fork in the narrow dirt road that led to the last bodega, the car was abandoned in the middle of some bushes, and as expected, I thought that they had gone into the bodega, so I went closer to the car and placed myself just behind some bushes waiting for them to come out again and find out what had happened. When about twenty minutes passed I thought they were probably having sex, so I thought about leaving. But, at that moment the guy appeared coming out of a corner of the funeral bodega, and went to his car, opened the trunk and took out a Truper box of tools. The moon was full that day so it was brightly lit and you could easily make out a face. And you'll never guess who it was in that black sedan," he said, as he paused again. This time Richard interrupted him.

-Come on, tell me who is...?

-Then he closed the trunk and just at that moment he dropped the keys, and he went to pick it up and when he did, the black cap fell in front of him. When he sat up again in the moonlight I could see his face... and... and it was him... Mr. President of the United States, Mr. Bill Sander..., yes it is him, the murderer... of those women," he said with a slight break in his voice due to the emotion that saying that meant to the man. At that very moment, Richard, in spite of the man's order, turned around completely stupefied, looked him in the eyes, kept an eternal silence and exclaimed.

- No, it can't be sir, it's a joke, right?

-Call me Artur," said the stranger with bald, black hair, whose apparently manly voice did not match the stranger's bearing, although he was obviously the same. At first glance, the guy was about 48 years old, slim and not very threatening. Although, Richard knew well that in real life appearances can be deceiving and you should never be taken in by someone's appearance.

- You gave me your word Mr. Richard, only this secret was killing me, I couldn't sleep. And I know I broke into your home, but..., it was the only way I could tell you this in safety, and forgive me for entering your home and pointing a gun at you....

- Don't worry, Mr. Artur," answered the detective, quite dismayed and at the same time incredulous of what the stranger was accusing the most powerful man in the world of, and that not even in his wildest dreams would he believe. And obviously, he was not going to believe, because he had the intuition that it was an alibi of the guy in front of him, who was still holding a nine millimeter.

-I can see in your face Mr. Richard that you don't believe me. You think it's a lie to get away with it, no no sir..., do you think I would have risked coming here for nothing, knowing I could get shot by you? Nooo, I'm no fool. But out there that Bill Sander guy is a psychopath and if he's not stopped he'll keep on killing. At the time, even I thought it was all a mistake, a mental pareidolia of mine, but no, when that guy went back inside that warehouse; I waited for him for several hours crouched there under the bushes .... I never imagined he would hurt him, I thought he wanted to have sex with a young girl and that was it, but hours later, he came out alone standing up from the back and a lump dragging and wow, it turned out to be Miss if I remember correctly Karla Davison. It was a human body. He struggled a few minutes for the weight with a total calmness in putting it in the front, then surely he removed the bag already inside, he felt safe to drive like that. About two hours from the reservation to the shopping center where he left him that night. I don't know the other victim that same morning, but he probably did it that night. What I'm telling you is true, it was the same black sedan, I'm not lying," he said a little more relaxed as silence fell, and not even Richard, who by that time had turned around and was sitting on the other party's armchair, could believe it. In his mind, it was impossible for the President to do that, since the secret service would prevent him from doing so and there was no way, theoretically according to him, to leave the White House without being guarded.

-His story seems credible," he commented suddenly. In his face he looked more condescending to Mr. Artur, who by that time had already been holding his gun under his jacket. Richard could have easily arrested him at that moment, since it was enough just to take out his gun and accuse him of everything, but he didn't do it. He approached him, looked at him closely and said, "Your story is disturbing, Mr. Artur, but you have my word that they will not know about you. I only want you to do one thing.

- What? -replied the astonished subject.

- To accompany me to the place of the events you are telling me about.

Artur hesitated for a second and then nodded, somehow that would give him more credibility, although it could also be dangerous even for Richard in case it was Artur's alibi and in reality he was the real murderer. But Richard thought that if he had wanted to kill him right there, he would have done it already. So they went that same evening to the place where the events of that victim had taken place.

# Something happened

The president of the United States, Mr. Bill Sander, had become president just a year ago with the majority of the votes in his favor, easily crushing his rival. Thanks to him, his party even won the majority in the Senate and the House of Representatives. Such was his charisma and results that there was talk that he could be one of the best presidents of the United States, even more than Ronald Reagan and more than Kennedy in charisma. The president was fifty-five years old when he took command of the most powerful country in the world. His intention was to be reelected, so he was making the best of his role before his people and the world. That is why he avoided at all costs getting involved in wars and solved everything through diplomatic channels.

For Richard to believe that stranger's confession seemed too bizarre. Bill's calm and altruistic personality was on another level. Never in his wildest nightmares would he imagine him murdering women, and even worse at night. His wife Melani Lamber, forty-five, was quite a beautiful and jovial woman and with her he made the perfect couple to please him in every way. So he found it hard to believe the story of a rapist president.

That same night the stranger and Richard went to the place. And sure enough, there was what he said. Arriving at the site by a dirt road, one could glimpse in the distance another small dirt road that led further to the bottom, to one side a last lamp post that illuminated the small construction of unfinished houses where Artur according to his confession served as "guard". The place was quite shady and full of wild vegetation on the sides. Right there began the nature reserve of all of western Columbia. In the background, four small warehouses with four or five stories each could be glimpsed. Both men went there with extinguished lamps in their hands, and in the fourth one, the farthest from the others, on the third floor, they found dried splashes of blood everywhere just in the corner of one of the cellars where it had been covered with leaves and garbage papers.

Undoubtedly the man had not lied. Now, it was just a matter of confirming that, although he had a plan and would not call forensics.

-Hey Arthur, I want you to help me with something," said Richard as he looked dimly at the stranger who was hesitantly looking down through the windows.

-I don't want to get involved in this anymore detective, I just want to leave, I already told you everything.

-I just want to ask you, will you still be working in that area?

-I don't think so, it's not convenient, they will surely suspect, but I'm going to Wisconsin. And you know, I don't want anyone to know, just in case who the whistleblower was," he refuted.

-Nothing will come out of me, don't worry. Well, if you won't work anymore because of all this, I don't know how to pay you, if you like to come with me to the house I'll give you something.

-No, I don't want money, it's enough that you do justice if you can.

The detective nodded, he knew that, if it was true, it would be the most disturbing case because of what it represented at the highest levels of power, but he would still have to carry it out, he could not back out, justice was justice. He said goodbye to the strange guy, although he did not trust him completely, he gave him the vote of doubt just in case. He left him on Maremont Avenue in the north of the city, and then disappeared down the avenue among dozens of passers-by. For Richard there was still the doubt that if the man he might never see again knew more or was the culprit, although his story had proof, it could also be a game, but he still had a plan.

Officially the investigations had come to a standstill, but he would continue unofficially with his friend Logan trying to catch the culprit red-handed. Once he told his partner Logan, he was stunned and just as incredulous at first he refused, but gradually he began to believe when he looked at some photos of the place where the girl had been tortured. And what could be observed to yet another by the excessive blood spatter in the corner near the second floor rear window. There were also bone splinters and they were clearly human.

**Richard Martel's house in the early hours of the morning hours later**

-Holy cow, I can't believe all this," Logan mumbled as he took a sip of water at Richard Martel's residence and they chatted about it. -Hey bro, are you sure this isn't a hoax by....

-You saw the photos, I went with the guy. If he had wanted to, he would have killed me, but he didn't and he trusted me. I already told you everything, so we'll go according to plan. I know it's risky, but there's no other way. I don't care that he's the most powerful man in the world, but if he goes around doing that he'll pay.

Logan looked at him doubtfully as if not believing what he was hearing.

-This doesn't make sense to me, no matter how many pictures you took, I don't think the president would leave the White House, just like that... the secret service would prevent it," he said.

-That's what I thought," Martel replied as he took a sip of coffee and looked warily toward the window at the back of the house.

-But President Bill doing that.... no no no no, I'm having a hard time wrapping my head around that one buddy.

-You never know what you're going to find in these cases. But, just in case, I hope he repeats the place again, because without proof we will not be able to accuse him, much less prove it. The big shots would annihilate us before trying. We know that psychopaths when they think they have a safe place to do their misdeeds repeat it, so we will wait for the entrance to that area tonight. Hopefully he will show up undetected and we will be able to stop him.

- If all this is true, I'm sure he'll do it again. It's becoming a vice," Logan mumbled. He was nervous because he knew it could be a dangerous thing, because to accuse the president even in infraganti and arrest him could easily be accused of kidnapping, charge them as perpetrators and send them to prison, and with the danger of being accused for the deaths of all the women and be sentenced to death. Besides, it would be the word of two detectives against the word of the most powerful man in the world.

# Unexpected ending

After those incidents Richard and Logan spent about a week waiting for the killer, whoever it was, to show up with a victim in that desolate place. In the first few days there were no results. But the murders just in that time frame continued with at least one more woman. A 27-year-old girl who went for a jog near Frederick Boulevard a few miles from where that first victim was found was found with the same tone of torture. Undoubtedly, the doer was the same. The same typical bar through the anus and exit through the mouth. So they deduced that in those days the guy must have had another place to torture, but true to what they had and knew, they had to play it safe until the guy was ready to go to them.

**And the unthinkable happened. On December 7, late at night.**

At one o'clock at night, a black 1987 Chevrolet Caprice began to enter at normal speed on that dirt road that led to those warehouses and to the area of the subdivision where the construction was stopped. That area was far away from the suburbs so it was quite lonely and where the weeds grew uncontrollably. The company Luvion Constructions, which started the subdivision and left it abandoned, had stopped work for more than a year, and it seemed that more would follow due to legal problems with the land. The federal reserve was only 100 meters away from the beginning, divided by 100 meters of bushes and wild vegetation.

Police officers Logan and Richard were waiting in the car in the foliage on the other side of the road. Right on the federal highway in front of the secondary dirt road that led to that area. They would keep their distance so that the subject who went there would not escape and they could arrest him in flagrante delicto, and if possible with film evidence. It was several minutes with the lights off until the Chevrolet was lost up ahead. After that, they also began to enter the dirt road. It wasn't more than five minutes on the rather battered road until they stopped exactly in the area where there should be a guard. But apparently the company had stopped guarding that area, as there was no sign of any guard. In order not to attract attention they left the car there, and carefully went through the back area of the subdivision to exit through the back of the buildings where they would continue straight on until they reached number four, which was probably where the Chevrolet car was. And indeed it was, the Chevrolet was parked exactly as the stranger had told him. They approached as close as possible, being cautious not to be seen from any of the windows on the second or third floor. They got as close as possible to the undergrowth, no more than three meters away. They realized that there was no one in the car. They were already inside whoever was accompanying that subject or subjects.

- What nerves," whispered Logan hesitantly, his face showing his fear of what they might find in there.

- I don't know if the story of that man who told me everything is true, but we have to go in," said Richard, reiterating that they would not tell anyone about the encounter with that stranger. - You know Tom, if we catch him we'll say that a guy called us on the phone and told us the place, and you know the rest.

Logan nodded a little nervously as he drew his nine millimeter pistol, Richard did the same, and with firm steps they began to approach the small warehouse building. At first glance there was only one entrance at the front and probably another at the back. But they immediately realized that the front metal doors were completely sealed with old welding, so they went out the back. Everything was dark at the beginning of the second floor. There were no noises on the second floor, everything was quiet. But those who entered should be on the upper floors.

Little by little they began to peek out and take the first steps inside. There was nothing on the second floor, only the remains of garbage. They did not want to illuminate the place with their lamps, in case there were more and alert them, but there was a certain uncertainty and fear in the air. They didn't know if the killer was armed, but he was clearly dangerous, and most likely he was, so they had to be careful.

They reached the middle of the building, just where the metal stairs leading to the second floor began. At that moment, a noise alerted them. It was as if someone was hammering something on the second level. Logan, somewhat alarmed, whispered at that moment;

-Do you think this...? - Richard said nothing and slowly began to climb the stairs that at best looked from the bottom like about twenty concrete steps with metal edges. He swallowed saliva and began to move forward carefully trying to make as little noise as possible. He knew that whoever was at the top had no escape, it was either die there or be stopped. He would not hesitate to shoot if they were attacked. The intention was to do justice as the law demanded. If it had been any other criminal, he would execute him there. But this case was very mediatic and they had to arrest whoever it was to psychologically leave a message of security to the city.

Just as he was about to pass halfway up the stairs the hammering stopped. Both of their hearts skipped a beat, already in itself because of the situation it signified. They knew someone was moving upstairs. Then a metal bar and some tools rang out, but there was no human sound to indicate that there were more people with the subject. Although Richard by this time feared the worst, that they had been late, and that the victim was dead. So, with extra courage he began to climb the next step. And when a minute later he made it, almost at the bottom he looked up. A guy in a black cap with his back completely turned was in mid-darkness doing a maneuver, right over a female corpse that could be glimpsed due to the moonlight hitting the window head-on, illuminating the scene luridly. The man in the black cap noticed the visitors because of the long shadows reflected on the floor by the light of the satellite. He did not turn around suddenly, but froze for a second. At that moment Richard shouted with authority:

-Don't move, put your hands where I can see them," Richard shouted in a firm tone as he pointed a gun to the head of the man dressed entirely in black. Logan looked around the room in the gloom in case there were more in the corners, and when he was sure that there was no one else, he said passively seconds later:

- Let's get our hands up.

But the guy ignored it, but he didn't try to escape either. Clearly, he knew he was in trouble. After standing still for a few seconds, he said in a hoarse voice:

-Come on agents, don't make this more difficult, how much money do you want?

Immediately Richard said. -I will have to shoot if you don't identify yourself and don't put your hands up... turn around with your hands up.

But just at that moment when he heard that order, he raised his hands, took off his cap and said to himself in a low tone, but with a boastful air: - I am the president of the United States, Mr. Bill Sander, and he looked them in the eyes with a countenance that was nothing like that noble, almost elderly president who in his speeches projected serenity and empathy towards everyone. He looked at them for a few seconds and smiled like a damned psychopath, while fresh blood dripped from his hands to the floor and gave more dread to the scene. Behind his back lay the unclothed female body of a female no more than thirty years old, totally violated and tortured, and just the scene showed the prelude when he was about to introduce the metal rod through her anus as the girl was in the Doggy Style sexual position.

Richard was stunned to see him face to face. He could not believe it. It seemed like a dream. The chief executive doing that was unthinkable, even witnessing it. But then the president said.

-I'm their boss, they can't stop me, they know that if I want I can call the secret service and accuse them," he answered cynically. Logan looked at his fearful partner and exclaimed in a low voice, "Hey Richard! He has power, it's a danger to stop him, let's get out of here.

-No.... I don't care that he's the president...he's sexually ill and goddamn ase...otherwise...I'll stop him.

-I am a lawyer before I am president and if I accuse you, you could spend the rest of your life in a cell, or be killed here by my boys... I just pick up the phone I have in my bag and tell them that I was kidnapped by two agents carrying a girl and that they are the culprits. They think they can take on the most powerful man in the world," I cynically rebutted as I smiled a nervous, but still totally cheeky, smile.

-If you put your hands down Bill trying to take your phone, I will shoot you, no one is above the law, not even you, so you will be brought to justice.

After seeing that Richard would not give in, neither for money nor for a better position that the president had proposed to him, he shouted in a furious tone: "You assholes... I see that you do not want to cooperate, good.

The president knew that even as powerful as he was, there were things he could not explain, and his alibi could get out of control if the media found out. So in despair he thought that his entire political and personal career would collapse, and he would go from being blameless to an evil, female-raping murderer. Therefore, he became brutally desperate.

-Why did he do it? -asked Richard suddenly.

-The president gave him a fleeting glance, then bowed his head, as if resigned. By that time he thought he could play the last card and try to make the call, and maybe his boys would arrive and kill the two inspectors, the problem was that if they let him.

-Inspector, I see that you are upright and honest, congratulations! -He then paused, and when Logan was about to approach him to handcuff him, he shouted:

-Wait wait, all right, I will cooperate, but..." he declared, paused again slightly and confessed. - I did it out of hatred... I feel a hatred towards them I don't know how to explain it, the demon enters at night, it takes over my mind... and I knew it was difficult to be president and continue with this.

-What? - said both detectives in chorus, undoubtedly that confession said a lot about his macabre plans and also about his past.

> — You're meaning damn it they're not the only ones
> you murdered in Columbia, you've got ...

The president interrupted him -yes.

-Since when? -asked the detective.

I don't know... I think since I became a lawyer about... twenty-six years ago.

That answer left both of them frozen.

-How many have you killed? -Logan asked hesitantly.

-I don't know, do the math," he answered coldly and cynically. Maybe that was his true personality that he didn't show to the public, and it was all a delusion of his mythomania. -You know, my stepmother as a child liked to humiliate and torture me in her own way, and maybe... That was something that triggered all this in me, I don't know, but it's not something I think about very much. I enjoy doing it, you can see that slut. -He pointed to the back where you could see a body barely visible. -It becomes a vice, and yes, despite my hatred towards them I abuse them to compensate my hatred, it's the only way that calms me down, it's like a drug....

-But why until now, Mr. Bill? I mean, you used to live in Illinois, and as far as I know there have never been any femicides of this nature... you've been in office for almost two years and this is the first time I've seen murders of this kind in Columbia...

He didn't answer for a few seconds, then said, "In Illinois it was much easier. When I wanted to be president inspector, I thought about leaving this psychopathy. But I know very well, I know that this thing I have is something impossible to resist, humanly I cannot. You don't know how many times I've tried not to murder, but... it's a feeling of ungovernable hatred," he said, raising his voice and bringing up a hand rubbing his face as if in desperation, then he ran them over his hair. And he kept them there as the order he had been given.

- In Illinois he buried them, in the small counties outside the city of Springfield, you know, beautiful young girls, and in all those decades they never suspected.

-You're a monster! I don't even have a definition for you," the chief detective replied in dismay.

- I'm not looking for that inspector, much less your approval, but you know...okay, I'll go with you, for today that's all I'll say, the whole statement I'll give before the judge.

- Mr. Bill anything you say from now on will be used for or against you, so keep your hands up. We will call the police and forensics. You are under arrest for the alleged murder of a person in the background, and the death of other suspects," said the inspector as he approached him. But three meters before he reached him, the president said in a raised voice. - Wait a second, there is another person.

Richard paused for a moment in thought and asked without thinking. - Who?

- The head of the secret service. Surely he was the one who gave you the information, he's a fucking traitor.

Richard thought of Artur. - "Artur he wasn't a guard then, it was he who".

- Surely he talked to you and told you. I'll be honest, I expected betrayal from someone, but less from him. I'll tell you, he also participated in the first victim. Maybe, it gave him some pangs of conscience and..., but you know, - he continued with an extraordinary calmness for having so much guilt that even the detective was stunned. And for what was coming, he looked quite calm.

-The head of the secret service is named Ron Brown, and I proposed this to him under threat, but then he gladly agreed. I gave him several thousand dollars a month, so he allowed me to leave the White House undetected by others. He supplied me with several cars, tools. Plus places. He would always go with me, well! He would go in another car watching my back, you know, there's always danger in such a big city. So surely he told you this place.

Richard shuddered, as he had suspected from the beginning that this guy had something to do with something, and he was clearly in on it too.

- Well Mr. Richard, my wife is my only regret for the suffering I will cause you. Fortunately we never had children to suffer for what is coming soon. Well detectives then...

As he lay resigned and defeated, Bill Sander ran directly towards the large, unprotected window behind him and threw himself into the void. Richard was unable to stop the action, but immediately called the police, who arrived on the scene.


On the ground the president's body lay without vital signs by the time both detectives arrived downstairs. They could have been charged if there had been no evidence, but fortunately the comparative DNA evidence found on the body of the first victims matched Bill Sander's hair, plus the multiple fingerprints found all over the area where he had tortured the bodies of several victims, plus the strong evidence of fresh semen traces on the last victim. Ron Brown, the one who had revealed everything and who had posed as Artur to Richard, was arrested weeks later and sentenced to life imprisonment for the participation and rape of Karla Davison, although he pleaded it, some traces of DNA were later discovered in the cellar.

The rejection, wave of disgust and repulsion towards the presidential figure was not long in coming days. Evidently, it was something historic in a presidential and political figure worldwide. Richard was decorated as Washington State Security Prosecutor for his great work towards public service, and for having solved the crime of the stranger, as the case had been initially called.

A few days later Richard was traveling through the state of Texas in his 1988 Camaro. He was speeding down that lonely highway, on the radio was playing: "The everybody hurts" by R.E.M. While he was humming the song, suddenly in the distance he looked at a girl who was hitchhiking, he looked in the rearview mirror and gave a little smile and then he was ready to stop. The girl was blonde and had a big smile, so it would be a nice ride to Houston where his destination was he thought.


**News Houston Texas 12 hours later 9 am**

In other news, a young woman was found murdered in the bushes, her body was raped and brutally tortured, the police believe it is a case of human trafficking, investigations are underway...

# Persecuted

"That's why I told you, Tom, that I didn't like excursions to remote villages away from civilization, but you didn't listen, huh? You were stubborn about coming here..."

"You can shut your damn mouth, Ale," Tom muttered under his breath, shrinking further amidst the foliage and wildflowers.

Tom and Ale had been married for 5 years, and due to a crisis in their marriage, he had suggested spending more time together. So, in the past few weeks, they had been exploring places near their hometown of Oregon. However, the previous week, Tom wanted to take it more seriously. He took a break to reconcile their marriage and booked a trip to a practically abandoned village in the eastern region of the Renier area in France. The village was surrounded by beautiful forests and lakes, making it the perfect place to rekindle their love.

Tom, a 35-year-old lawyer from the eastern area of Portland, was completely captivated when he met Ale, who was 10 years younger than him. But as is often the case in most marriages, monotony tends to extinguish that spark if nothing is done about it. Their dreams were shattered because Ale wanted to have three beautiful children, but Tom always had reservations due to work. He wanted to enjoy more time as a couple before having children. However, this gradually drove them apart to the point that they were on the verge of divorce in the past year. Amidst fights and Tom's lack of interest, Ale decided to separate a few weeks ago. Fearing to lose her, Tom planned all these outings as a couple in an attempt to save their crumbling marriage. Surprisingly, it seemed to be working over the past few weeks, especially when he told her they were going to France.

But now a couple of days have passed, and our dear couple finds themselves in a rather strange situation.

"You were the one who wanted children, but do you know what that means? more expenses, more..."

"Shut up, coward," she interrupted in a whisper. "If I had known about this, I would have never married you. Do you even know what marriages are for?"

Tom didn't respond; his eyes only wandered from here to there, as if trying to see beneath the paths in that wooded area. She continued.

"Marriages are for having children or doing things together, but you've only been working and working, but for..."

"They're going to find us. Just calm down! This is not the time for these discussions, Ale."

"What does it matter, huh?" she replied in a sarcastic tone.

"It's not easy, Ale, to have children, and you know, it means a lot of things," he added, not really caring about that topic at that moment. But knowing Ale and her paranoia and tantrums, she was capable of causing a scene there and getting them discovered.

"You know, Jada, who went to secondary school with me, just had her third child, and her husband knows how to take care of her. I wish I had met a man like that!"

This time, Tom didn't say anything; he just remained silent. Because at that moment, what mattered was getting out of that place by any means necessary.

Suddenly, something started to be heard in the distance. Ale, at that moment, realized once again that this was not a dream; it was completely real. Arguing about relationship issues and such was not important in those minutes. The important thing was their safety.

-Forgive me, Tom, I'm scared," she said suddenly. Tom glanced at her briefly, and she approached him, hugging him. Still a little annoyed, he let go of his anger and hugged her back with one hand.

"What do they want from us, Tom? I..." she didn't finish the sentence as he covered her mouth with his hand.

"Shhh, don't move," Tom whispered almost under his breath. Then he directed her gaze downward, about fifteen meters away, hidden by vegetation.

"Oh my goodness! Who are they? Tom, I don't want..." she whispered, stuttering, and continued, "Are they the same ones who chased us on the road?"

"Silence, Ale. Don't move," her husband ordered. Ale covered her mouth with her hands to stifle a scream of panic.

Underneath them were four individuals, each holding an axe in their hands, wearing homemade masks resembling crows, as if made from the skin of some strange animal. The figures moved their heads in all directions, trying to find them.

Faced with that sight, Tom and Ale remained motionless for a few minutes until the individuals seemed to leave the area.

"The night is falling, love, we have to go," Ale said after an hour of silence.

"It seems like they're gone," her husband replied, somewhat pensive, for he didn't want to die. The truth was that Tom had never told his wife why he didn't want to have children. The main reason behind it was his infertility. When he promised her children during their brief courtship, he said that because he loved her and didn't want to lose her to Lucas, a businessman who courted her in those years.

Tom got up from the ground, quickly scanning their surroundings, and said, "Let's wait for about twenty minutes until the light completely fades, and then we'll walk downhill. Maybe we'll reach a nearby village."

"Honey, if only we could go to the car, the map is there," Ale replied, obviously speaking hypothetically.

Tom shook his head. "That would be suicide... The only way to get out alive is to walk downstream along the river." His wife nodded in agreement.

Both of them had arrived in that supposedly abandoned village through an internet advertisement. Out of the two hundred cottages that extended along a kilometer, almost all were deserted and weathered by time, except for a small hotel still in operation. It was the only place where the few tourists who came there each month usually spent the nights. The hotel consisted of six old rooms. The caretaker was an elderly man with one eye, his elderly wife, and a mute daughter. The first two days were spent exploring the surroundings, especially the beautiful crystalline lakes. Only on the third day did they decide to venture into the wooded mountains of that paradise.

But something happened on the night of October 3rd that turned their trip into a nightmare.

After a while, the couple started going downhill towards a river that was perhaps a kilometer away at most. They were walking briskly and swiftly. Tom had a rock in his left hand and a piece of wood in his right hand, ready to strike anyone who stood in their way. They moved through the undergrowth, careful not to make any noise or attract attention in case those damn guys were around...

"At least the moon is up, otherwise we wouldn't be able to walk," Ale whispered beside him. He heard her, but didn't say anything, he was focused on the path ahead. After a while, they finally reached the river and crossed it without hesitation. It wasn't a time to worry about getting their clothes wet since the weather was pleasant, and the humidity actually helped instead of being a hindrance.

They walked tirelessly for hours until late into the night when they were exhausted. Finally, they spotted a couple of small houses in the distance. Both of them were overjoyed because they had already walked at least thirty kilometers and had only rested for a couple of hours throughout the night; this was more than they could have hoped for.

"Do you see it, my love?" Tom exclaimed, filled with happiness. She looked into his eyes and gave him a big hug. It was the best thing they could do in that situation.

Without wasting time, they started jogging to reach the houses as soon as possible. In their thoughts, that experience had somehow brought them closer together. Despite her constant criticisms of him, he never abandoned her in that place, and that had deeply touched Ale, making her love him even more. When they finally approached the nearest adobe house, they didn't hesitate to knock. It seemed like someone in that house woke up very early. It was perhaps four in the morning, and smoke was already rising from the chimney in the distance.

"Hello, hello, is anyone here?" Tom shouted a bit loudly, followed by Ale and both of them doing the same. But they received no response. Without wasting time, they walked about ten meters to the next house, with the same result. However, it should be noted that the second house was completely dark, so they returned to the house with smoke coming from the chimney. After a few minutes, feeling a bit desperate, Tom turned the doorknob since he felt confident enough to open it. At that point, it didn't matter. Lost in the middle of nowhere and having survived some damn lunatics, opening a door was inconsequential.

"What are you doing, love?"

"They probably already left for work," Tom replied.

The fact was that the house wasn't very big, judging by three rustic rooms and a kitchen. He then opened the old wooden door a little and stepped inside. When he looked to his left, he was completely dumbfounded and couldn't believe it. There were a couple of dismembered bodies on a large, antique wooden table. Tom froze, and Ale noticed it, asking him:

"What's wrong, love? Why aren't you coming in? What are you looking at?" He turned around in horror, barely managing to utter a voice from his throat, while looking at her with wide eyes filled with shock. "They're here." When he finished saying that, about fifteen masked figures started approaching from around the houses, similar to the ones from the previous night.

Both of them started embracing tightly. At that moment, Tomas realized everything; this was the end. There was no way to fight against it. After a few moments, one of those figures, the smallest one, stopped about eight meters away from them and slowly removed his crow mask. Then, to their astonishment, it was incredible. Before them stood the innkeeper from the hotel.

"Why are you doing this, sir? What have we done to you?" The one-eyed old man turned to the men who came with him, then started laughing before uttering, "It's nothing personal, but the flesh tastes good...

Quote

"In the dark of night, a chilling silence grips the neighborhood. The deserted streets become the stage for a macabre dance. Hiding in the shadows is a bloodthirsty serial killer, whose name and face are an enigma to all. Stealthy and calculating, the killer stalks his victims, carefully selecting those who least suspect their terrible fate. His steps follow a sinister choreography, pursuing his prey with the certainty that no one will be safe. The authorities are baffled, unable to discover the identity of the monster lurking in the darkness. Meanwhile, the city is plunged into terror, every corner becomes a death trap and every glance hides danger. The inhabitants live in fear, not knowing when or where the next attack will be. In this macabre dance of blood and horror, everyone wonders who will be the next to fall into the clutches of the faceless serial killer, immersed in a relentless terror that gives no respite."

**52**

End